I

SGP
STORMGATE PRESS

stormgatepress.com
stormgatepress@gmail.com

Copyright © 2024 by Charles F. Millhouse
All rights reserved. This book or any portion thereof may not be reproduced or used in any manner whatsoever without the express written permission of the publisher except for the use of brief quotations in a book review or scholarly journal.
First Printing: 2024
ISBN: 9798343705157
Imprint: Independently published

Introducing the Stormgate Press Quick Read Books

Short Story Pulp Adventure Books
Reminiscent of the dime store novels of old.

BOOK 1: The Purple Mystique

BOOK 2: Night Vision

BOOK 3: A Zane Carrington Adventure

BOOK 4: The Purple Mystique: Purple Incognito

BOOK 5: Zane Carrington: The Contract

BOOK 6: Tales From the Other Side of the World: The Barbarian With No Name.

BOOK 7: Zane Carrington: Eternity's Time Clock

BOOK 8: Night Vision: Death Takes a Number (coming soon).
Watch for more books in the series coming soon...

SGP STORMGATE PRESS — MAKING READING FUN AGAIN!

A STORMGATE PRESS QUICK READ BOOK

NIGHT VISION

CHARLES F. MILLHOUSE

Purple Incognito
Charles F. Millhouse

PART I

The fog rolled in thick off Lake Michigan, shrouding the streets of Chicago in a ghostly haze. The lamplights struggled to pierce the mist; their light caught in the eerie haze. It was a city of whispers, and secrets, where the night concealed much more than it revealed. And somewhere in this sprawling metropolis, the Purple Mystique was on the prowl.

Through the fog ladened streets, her purple Bentley moved through the dark. Behind the wheel sat Danny Brocko a broad-shouldered man with a square jaw and rustic brown eyes, Danny was more than just a chauffeur; he was her confidant, her protector, the only soul privy to the secrets that lay beneath the brim of her hat.

"Are you sure about this?" Danny asked.

"It has to be tonight," Mystique replied in a soft but determined tone. "It's the one chance I have to turn the tide in this mission against Bobby Two Tone. Besides, they won't be expecting this, they think they're safe in the den of thieves. I'm about to prove them wrong."

Danny remained silent. He knew that when the Purple Mystique had a plan it wasn't wise to try and talk her out of it. "Are you sure you don't want backup with this one?"

There was a hint of laughter from the back of the car, and Mystique said, "You're good, Danny. But you do your best work hiding in plain sight."

Danny's eyes smiled in the rearview mirror as a streetlight flickered over them. As a leg man for the city's prosecutor, Danny had worn many hats, been many people to fit into any given situation. From a reporter for the Chicago Defender, to streetwise taxicab driver Elias Hornsby and prize fighter Danny "The Kid" Brocko. In his many personas Danny kept the pulse of the city close, supplying the Purple Mystique with information in her one-woman war. Although dangerous, Danny saw it as a small price to pay to help rid the streets of crime that plagued the city.

The Bentley came to a stop near the harbor sometime after midnight, the sound of tugboats whistled in the distance and shouts of overnight dock workers could be heard giving each other the razz, admits laughter.

"Keep an eye out," Mystique said as she stood outside the driver's side door.

THE PURPLE MYSTIQUE

"I always do," Danny replied. "One last chance. You sure you want to do this tonight? I mean it's so soon after the last bloody nose you gave Boyce."

"That's exactly why we are out here tonight. We can't allow Two Tone to think for even a minute that he is safe from me," The Mystique said as she slipped through the shadows, her every movement calculated and precise.

The guards outside the warehouse never saw the Purple Mystique coming. She dispatched them with ease, a flash of purple in the darkness, a gloved hand delivering a knockout blow before they could even cry out. Keeping her neutralizer safely concealed in the folds of her coat, she didn't need to bring attention to herself by expelling the amethyst gas. The hypnotic neurotoxin that bends the will of its victims. Comprised of a special strain from the Malva Sylvestris plant in Southeast Asia, Mystique learned of its potency while on a visit to China in 1926.

Concealing the two guards behind oversized crates, the Purple Mystique stealthily entered the warehouse. Inside, she found a maze of crates and barrels, the air thick with the smell of oil and saltwater. Two Tone's men were everywhere, but the Mystique moved among them like a wraith, slipping between the crates, an enigma. Coming at them in a frontal assault would be a mistake. She might be enigmatic, but a bullet would kill her, as easily as it would any other. She would conceal herself, and strike at them like a viper; with stealth and precision.

Withdrawing into a hiding place, Mystique discovered a crowbar resting atop a crate. Scooping it up into her hand, she withdrew into the darkness of her nook, rapping the end of the metal tool on the floor in front of her. The footfalls quickened, heading in her direction. When a black suited man came near her, she coiled up her fist and struck like a viper.

Coming out of the shadows in an amethyst blur, the henchman barely had time to turn toward her as Mystique drew back on the crowbar – throwing weight into her swing, clobbering the gangster across the face in a furious *whack*. The man spun in a complete circle before his legs went out from under him and he toppled to the floor.

Not taking time to admire her work, the Purple Mystique crossed into another avenue of crates, skirting along them at a quickened pace. It wouldn't be long before that man came up missing, and she needed to be prepared for more of Two Tone's men as they came searching for her.

"Over here!" she heard a man shout. His cry was serious and filled with rage. Seconds later the clammer of winged tipped shoes scuffled across the floor as someone yelled, "Spread out."

Discarding the crowbar, Mystique brought out her neutralizer. If she was to face a hoard of men, she needed to even her chances. Having trained in Asian fighting techniques, she could hold her own against one, two or even three men, but more than that would be tempting fate, and with her mission far from over, she couldn't risk being stopped. Not now. Not when her war on Bobby Boyce was just getting started.

THE PURPLE MYSTIQUE

Keeping to the shadows, she would wait, refraining from seeking out the gangsters looking for her. If she could get a clean enough shot at the bulk of the men in the warehouse, she could turn the tides on them.

When a seething hiss came out of the darkness, a large and imposing black man appeared from the shadows, grabbing Mystique by the back of the neck and tossing her several feet. When she hit the floor, she lost the hold on the neutralizer, and it slid out of her reach. Heavy footfalls came at her and before the Purple Mystique could get back to her feet the large man was upon her.

Using the skills bestowed upon her by a remarkable Chinese man named, Bai, Mystique put her body into motion. Turning onto her back, she spun herself clockwise, using her powerful legs as a weapon, strafing the large man in a sweeping motion, knocking him off his kilter long enough for her to get back to her feet.

The impressive man charged Mystique, rage in his dark eyes. With her fists up in front of her, she dodged his first swing and his second, but the third knocked her oversized fedora off her head, exposing her delicate features to her attacker.

Stunned for a second, as if the man recognized her, he cleared his thoughts, and reached out for her, but the Purple Mystique used his confusion to her advantage, building power into her arms, she threw a tight fist clobbering the henchman in the face.

Stunned, the man stumbled back, but despite her fury, it wasn't enough to send the man to the floor, but it did give Mystique time to scoop up the neutralizer. She turned, pressed the trigger and expelled the amethyst gas shrouding the ebony skinned man in purple fog.

Having built up an immunity to the regal vapor, Mystique scooped up her fedora placed it back on her head and approached the henchman who stood glary eyed into oblivion. "Listen to me," Mystique said. "You didn't see my face, you don't know who I am, and you will not remember who I am. Do you understand?"

"The gangster signified his understanding with a nod.

"Good," Mystique said adding satisfaction to her voice. "You will find a hiding place, and you will not come out until daybreak, do you understand?"

Again, the man nodded an understanding.

"Go," she said, now with more authority in her tone, and she watched the man follow his instructions.

Before she could recenter herself, Mystique heard the approaching men in the warehouse, and she spun when they came into view.

"It's the Purple Mystique…!" one of the men yelled.

They charged her, and even though Mystique expelled more toxin into the air, two of the men came out of the mist preparing for a fight. Mystique went low, throwing a punch to the midsection of the man closest to her. He bellied over, but when he straightened himself, his eyes were clouded in violet.

"Protect me," Mystique ordered, and the spellbound man reacted, clobbering his compatriot who came through the mist with him, sending him to the floor. When the amethyst gas dissipated, the remaining men stood enthralled. Under her control Mystique ordered, "Go to sleep, sleep until tomorrow night and you will remember nothing of what you saw here."

One by one, they fell to the floor, curling up like newborn babies. Satisfied, Mystique turned her attention to the flight of stairs and the warehouse office.

Entering the office with her weapon in front of her, Mystique found Angelo "Sweet Face" Carmine alone. The heavyset man was struck unprepared – a cigar clenched between his teeth. "The Purple Mystique," he snarled, though the fear in his voice was unmistakable. The Mystique didn't answer. Instead, she stepped into the room, the brim of her hat casting a shadow over her face.

Carmine reached for the revolver on his desk, but Mystique was faster, reaching the weapon before him. "W-what do you want?" Carmine stammered, his bravado crumbling as he realized he was facing the one person in the city who couldn't be bribed or intimidated. The Mystique pointed to the corner of the room, where a large ledger lay on a small table. Carmine followed her gaze, confusion knitting his brow. "That? You want the ledger?" he asked nervously.

The Mystique gave a single nod. For a moment, Carmine seemed to consider his options, but he knew there were none. "Two Tone will kill me, if I let you take that," he said.

"And I will do far worse to you if you don't," Mystique promised.

Carmine was trapped, and by the look on his face he knew it. "Don't play games with me Sweet Face," Mystique warned. "I'm not in the mood for it."

With a resigned sigh, Carmine picked up the ledger and handed it to her. As the Mystique took the book, she spared him one last glance. There was no pity in her eyes, only cold, calculating judgment.

Carmine froze, fear etched his features. He understood in a very few short hours, he would be dead, another victim of Bobby "Two Tone" Boyce. "Before he does you in," Mystique said. "I want you to tell him, this is just the beginning. There will be no place he can hide, no place he can run, where I won't see him brought to justice."

"Why would I do you a favor? What's in it for me?"

"Who knows," Mystique replied. "Bobby might go easy on you and give you a crack at me."

"You better hope he doesn't," Carmine warned. "The next time, I'll put a bullet in you."

Without a reply, Mystique turned and left, disappearing into the shadows as quickly as she had appeared.

***

When the Purple Mystique returned to the Bentley, Danny was waiting, as always. He didn't ask any questions as she slid into the backseat, and he started the engine and drove away, leaving the warehouse behind. As they drove through the fog-drenched streets of Chicago, Danny couldn't help but glance at the Mystique in the rearview mirror. She was holding the ledger, her gloved fingers tracing the cover. He knew what was inside—names, dates,

THE PURPLE MYSTIQUE

details of every dirty deal Two Tone had ever made. With that book, the Mystique could dismantle his entire empire.

But Danny also knew that the ledger was just the beginning. The war against the underworld was far from over, and the Mystique would not rest until every last one of them had been brought to justice. As they approached the city's edge, the fog began to thin, and the first light of dawn crept over the horizon. The Purple Mystique removed her hat, allowing the cool morning air to brush against her face. Danny caught a glimpse of her in the rearview mirror, but only for a moment before she turned away. He didn't need to see her face to know the determination that burned within her. It was the same determination that drove her night after night, through danger and darkness, with only him by her side. The Bentley disappeared into the early morning light, leaving behind a city still sleeping, still unaware of the battle being fought in its shadows. And somewhere in the heart of Chicago, Bobby "Two Tone" Boyce learned of her victory this night, and he knew that the Purple Mystique was coming for him again. It was only a matter of time.

PART II

Twenty-four hours later, across Chicago on Lake Shore Drive in the midst of a steady rain, the sound of music jamming from inside the walls of the city most prominent night club filled the street. The neon sign outside the Silver Key flickered with a hazy glow, casting an orange hue over the wet pavement. Inside, the air was thick with smoke and the low hum of jazz emanated from the stage where Lena "Velvet" Thompson was just wrapping up her set. Her voice, sultry and smooth, lingered in the air as the last note fell. She was the kind of woman who could draw the attention of a room just by breathing and tonight was no different.

Danny Brocko watched her from a corner booth, half-hidden in shadow, his fedora tipped low over his eyes. Though his involvement with The Purple Mystique was a mystery. It was wise to keep his presence on the down low considering Bobby Boyce owned the Silver Key. If anything, he wasn't here for the music, though Lena had a voice that could make a man forget his troubles. No, tonight was about something far more dangerous than a broken heart or a misplaced drink. As Lena finished, the scattered applause of the audience seemed to barely registered with her. She gave a small, practiced smile and slipped off the stage, heading straight for Danny's booth as if she knew he was there all along.

"Danny," she purred – her olive skin sheened with sweat. Sliding into the seat opposite him she reached out and placed her hand on top of his. Her eyes darting about the audience as they settled back into their seats as the next performer began their show. Her dark eyes sparkled with a knowing gleam, though what she knew, Danny wasn't about to guess. "What's the word on the street?" she asked allowing the music to conceal her words.

"Not much," Danny replied. "I figured there would be heightened security everywhere, including this place."

"Bobby's been in a mood tonight. Word is the Purple Mystique hit him pretty hard."

THE PURPLE MYSTIQUE

Danny allowed himself a small smile. "I wouldn't know anything about that," he said. "Besides, Bobby's always in a mood."

"Not like this," Lena countered, leaning forward slightly. Her perfume was subtle, but it had a way of invading the senses, making it hard to think of anything else. "He's fit to be tied. If the information in that ledger hits the streets, it could cause him a great deal of trouble."

"Is it going to hit the street?" Danny asked.

Taken back by the question, Lena said with a devilish smile, "Hell if I know. But it would bring his criminal empire down like a house of cards."

Danny remained silent, letting her words hang in the air between them. Lena wasn't one to waste breath on idle chatter. Especially when it came to Bobby "Two Tone" Boyce.

"You know Bobby's temper," Danny said finally, as if brushing away a bothersome fly. "Always looking for someone to blame when things go wrong. Are you going to be safe here?"

"I always am," Lena said. "He suspects nothing."

"That you know of," Danny replied. "You stay safe, I'm not always around to protect you."

"My safety isn't the concern. Seeing that Bobby pays for his wrongs, is," Lena said, her eyes flashed with something—was it mischief, or was it a warning?

"We both know how this game works." Danny said drumming his fingers on the table nervously. The game where if you know too much, you disappear. And a lot of people have disappeared since Bobby came to power."

Lena met his gaze, unflinching. "I knew the game when I started playing. I know the risks," she assured him. "What Two Tone did to me is unforgivable. I won't rest until he's put away for a very, very long time. So, you see, I know how the game works."

"Some people are better at playing it than others," Danny replied as the song ended and applause filled the night club.

As the next song began, the two of them sat in silence, the unspoken words filling the space between them. Danny could feel the weight of the conversation pressing down on him, but he couldn't let it show. Not here. Not with her.

"I just don't like it, is all," Danny said. "You're playing this too close. Sooner or later, he's going to become wise."

"Bobby's a lot of things, but he's not stupid," Lena continued after a beat. "He's got his suspicions."

"He always does," Danny replied smoothly. "But that doesn't mean they're right."

Lena smiled faintly, a shadow of something darker behind her eyes. "No, it doesn't. But it makes things… interesting, don't you think?" Danny didn't answer. He couldn't afford to. The fewer words he said, the less he'd have to take back later. Lena was a sharp one, he trusted her – he always did.

"You've always had a knack for finding yourself in the middle of interesting situations," Danny said.

"Funny how that keeps happening."

"Funny," Danny agreed, his voice flat.

"Still," Lena leaned in closer, her voice dropping to a near whisper. "We can't take any chances. It might be best

THE PURPLE MYSTIQUE

if you don't come around here for a while. We need to distance ourselves, and only meet when necessary."

Danny tucked the fedora tight on his head and slid out of the booth. "Be careful, Bobby's not someone you want to cross."

"I'm far past that," Lena replied. "I'll call you when and if I need you."

Standing, Danny turned to see Bobby "Two Tone" Boyce brazen into the night club with an entourage of heavy hitters. On his tail was the beautiful Rosalind DuBois, known to everyone as Bobby's dame. But by her expression, when Rosie caught sight of Danny Brocko there was an instant connection. She offered him an explicit glance not to draw attention to himself. Anyone caught looking at Rosie for more than a second brought an instant reprisal from Two Tone.

Lena slid out of the booth and straightened her dress, smoothing out invisible wrinkles. Drawing Danny's attention to her, she asked, "You know Bobby's woman?"

Danny refrained from replying. Sometimes, keeping secrets from those closest to you, was the only way to protect them. Besides, he was already waist-deep in the mess brewing, and keeping himself focused on that was better than trying to explain what Rosie meant to him. It was just one more piece of a puzzle, another secret he had to keep.

***

Bobby "Two Tone" Boyce stood by the wide bay window in his private suite, the neon glow from the sign outside flickered through the glass. His hand gripped a half-empty glass of bourbon, the ice clinking as he brought it to his lips. The city sprawled out before him, a maze of shadows and deceit, but none of that concerned him tonight. Tonight, his fury was confined to this room.

"Where were you last night, Rosie?" Bobby's voice was low, dangerous, as he turned to face the woman lounging on the velvet chaise behind him.

Rosalind "Rosie" DuBois looked up from the magazine she'd been pretending to read, her dark eyes locking onto his. Her expression was carefully composed, but there was a flicker of something in her gaze – something Bobby couldn't quite place. "I told you, Bobby," she replied, her voice soft and sweet, with just a hint of something else, "I was with the girls, down at the club. We had a few drinks, listened to the band... nothing special."

Bobby took a slow step toward her, his gaze never leaving hers. "That so? Funny, 'cause I heard there was some trouble at the docks last night, and your car was parked five blocks from there."

"I didn't say I stayed with the girls all night. I had too much to drink, too much and I couldn't drive. I pulled over until my head cleared. You know how I get."

"Yeah," Bobby said in a dubious tone.

"I must have gotten lost, I had no idea I was near the docks," Rosie said.

"I got hit by that troublesome broad, the Purple Mystique, last night." He snarled. "She took something rather important to me... something I need back."

Rosie's eyes widened slightly, but she kept her composure, setting the magazine aside. "The docks? Bobby,

THE PURPLE MYSTIQUE

you know I don't get mixed up in your business. I told you I was sleeping it off."

Bobby studied her, searching for any sign of deceit, any crack in her armor. But Rosie was a pro, always had been, that's what had drawn Bobby to her in the first place. She was cool under pressure, always a step ahead. But lately, she'd been too cool, too distant. And with that damned vigilante, the Purple Mystique, tearing his operations apart piece by piece, Bobby's paranoia had reached a boiling point.

"You better not be lying to me, Rosie," he warned, his voice a growl. "If I find out you had anything to do with what happened last night, it won't end well for you."

Rosie stood, smoothing her dress, the deep crimson fabric hugging her curves as she walked over to him. She placed a hand on his chest, her touch light but firm. "Bobby, you know you can trust me. I'd never cross you. Whoever this Purple Mystique is, they've got nothing to do with me. Besides, do I look like a gal who would dress in god-awful purple and fight men a size and a half larger than me?"

Bobby cracked a smile. He wanted to believe her. Hell, a part of him did. But another part, the part that had been burned too many times before, wasn't so sure. Bobby grabbed her wrist, pulling her close, his breath hot against her ear. "Don't make a fool out of me, Rosie," he whispered, his grip tightening.

She winced slightly but didn't pull away. "I wouldn't dream of it, baby." He released her, turning away with a curse, hurling the empty glass across the room. It shattered against the wall, the sound echoing through the suite like a gunshot. Rosie didn't flinch.

A knock at the door interrupted the tense silence. Bobby's jaw clenched as he barked, "Come in!" The door opened to reveal Angelo "Sweet Face" Carmine, his face pale and drawn. The nickname Sweet Face was a cruel irony, a relic of his boyhood. Now, with his broken nose, sunken eyes, and pockmarked skin, he was anything but sweet.

Bobby pointed a finger at Angelo as he approached, his eyes narrowing. "You better have some good news for me, Angie."

Angelo swallowed hard, his hands trembling slightly as he wrung them together. "I... I don't, Bobby. The ledger... it's gone. That damn Mystique got it before I could stop 'er. But I swear, I'm gonna get it back. Just give me some time."

Bobby's face darkened, and he moved with sudden speed, grabbing Angelo by the collar and slamming him against the wall. "Time? You want time? I don't have time, Angelo! That ledger's got everything in it—names, numbers, every deal I've made in the last six months! If it gets out, we're all dead!"

Angelo choked on his words, his eyes wide with fear. "I-I know, Bobby, I know! But I'm telling you, I'll find it. I've got some guys on it already. We'll track down the Mystique and make 'er pay."

Bobby let go of Angelo with a snarl, shoving him away. "You better, or the Mystique will be the least of your problems."

THE PURPLE MYSTIQUE

Angelo stumbled, straightening his jacket with trembling hands. "I won't let you down, Bobby. I swear."

Bobby turned his back on Angelo, pacing the room like a caged tiger. His mind raced, a storm of rage and suspicion. He couldn't shake the feeling that someone close to him was playing both sides. Maybe Angelo was in on it, maybe Rosie... hell, maybe the whole damn city was against him. But he couldn't afford to let his paranoia get the best of him. Not yet. He needed to keep his focus, keep his enemies close, and his secrets even closer.

"Get outta here, Angie," Bobby finally growled. "And don't come back until you've got that ledger in your hands." Angelo didn't need to be told twice. He practically sprinted for the door, leaving Bobby and Rosie alone once more.

The suite felt colder now, the walls closing in, the darkness outside pressing against the windows like a living thing. Rosie watched Bobby carefully as he poured himself another drink, her expression unreadable.

"Bobby... what are you gonna do?"

He didn't answer immediately, just took a long, slow sip of bourbon, letting the warmth spread through him, dulling the edge of his fury. "I'm gonna find the bitch who's been screwin' with me, Rosie. And when I do... she's gonna wish she'd never been born."

Rosie nodded, her eyes dark and inscrutable. "And what if it's someone you trust?" Bobby looked at her sharply, her words cutting through his haze of anger.

"What are you trying to say, Rosie?"

She shook her head, a small, sad smile playing at her lips. "Nothing, Bobby. Just... be careful."

He stared at her for a long moment, searching her face for any sign of betrayal, but found none. Rosie was as cool as ever, an enigma wrapped in silk and secrets. And that's what kept Bobby up at night—because in this city, trust was a luxury he couldn't afford.

***

The following morning, Danny hammered his fist on the office door of Prosecutor William Hartwell and opened it sticking his head in, "You wanted to see me, Boss?"

William Hartwell sat behind his desk, clutching a phone receiver to his ear. He waved Danny in, his piercing blue eyes focusing intently as he spoke on the phone.

Danny placed his fedora on a table near the door and then perched on the edge of a worn leather chair facing Hartwell's desk. Danny's no stranger here, he's Hartwell's leg man, his go-to for the dirty work that never makes it to the courtroom.

Danny began working for Hartwell after a chance meeting at a local bar. Danny, known citywide for his achievements as a prize fighting boxer, wanted to put his streetwise talents to work fighting for justice in the Windy City, and Hartwell recognized Danny's potential and determination, and offered him a job working for him. This opportunity marked the start of Danny's career, where he quickly proved himself through hard work and dedication, earning the respect of the D.A.

A sharp-witted man in his mid-fifties Hartwell's broad shoulders carried the weight of a man in his prime. His graying hair, meticulously combed, framed a face carved by years of relentless pursuit of justice, his piercing blue eyes flicking back and forth in their sockets as his conversation ended. "Yes, yes, I'll see to that, goodbye," he said hanging up the phone.

There was a moment of silence before Hartwell said, "So, Sweet Face slipped up. What's the word on the street?"

"He might have slipped up," Danny said sliding into the aged leather chair. "But from what I've learned, Boyce gave him another chance. He wants Sweet Face to find and retrieve the ledger stolen from him by the Purple Mystique."

The expression on Hartwell's face twisted in disgust. "The Purple Mystique? Seems the world is filling up with these vigilante types."

Danny offered a serious look, often wondering what Hartwell would think of him for secretly working with the Purple Mystique. When Hartwell tossed a newspaper on the desk in front of Danny, he said, "Seems New York has their own troublesome vigilante."

Leaning forward, Danny read the headline: *NEW YORK PROWLED BY THE NIGHT VISION*. "Is this real?" he asked.

"As real as the Purple Mystique it would seem," Hartwell said.

At that moment, the office door opened, and Barbara Hartwell came into the room. As she stepped into the office, her presence commanded attention. Her long, shapely legs were accentuated by the silk stockings, and the blue dress she wore, highlighting her curves, complementing her fair complexion. Her dark hair cascaded in soft waves. She carried herself with an air of confidence, though the high heels seemed to betray a hint of discomfort. Her eyes sparkled with intelligence and determination, suggesting a woman who knew her worth and wasn't afraid to assert herself. As she moved, there was a gracefulness to her stride, despite the challenges of her footwear. With a warm smile that could light up a room, she exuded a blend of professionalism and charisma, she flashed Danny a curious eye, disregarding him as quickly as she looked away.

"You're here earlier than I expected," Hartwell said. "Our lunch date isn't until twelve-thirty."

"I was bored at home, and thought I'd come into the city a bit early," Barbara said sitting on the edge of her father's desk. "Am I interrupting something?"

"Just business," Hartwell said.

Barbara glanced at Danny. "Two Tone again?" she asked.

"You know I can't tell you that," Hartwell replied.

"He should have been thrown behind bars years ago," Barbara said with disdain. Her hatred ran deep for Bobby "Two Tone" Boyce, after he gunned down her mother in the street seven years ago. "How he's been able to remain free all this time is beyond me."

"We've talked about this, Barbara..."

"I know, politics. I don't see how that would interfere with bringing a man to justice," Barbara said glancing at the newspaper on the desk before sharing a look with Danny, and then shoved the paper away dismissively.

"It's more to it than that," Hartwell said. "The fight for justice takes time, but that doesn't mean we won't win, *we will*. But unlike those we are fighting to get off the streets, we have rules to follow, even though the hoods we are fighting against don't. That just makes our victories a bit sweeter."

"Well, I think Justice takes too long," Barbara said with disdain. "Sometimes vengeance is a bit sweeter."

"Now you sound like that trench coat vixen, the Purple Mystique," Hartwell said, and he pulled out his pipe from the desk and began filling it with a sweet tobacco. "She's only causing more problems than she's helping."

"Maybe she thinks what's she's doing is right," Barbara said with a lilt of certainty in her voice. "You don't have to get mad about it."

"I'm not mad," Hartwell replied.

Barbara chuckled, and said, "When you get angry you fill your pipe, even though you gave up smoking it years ago."

Hartwell offered a smile. "I'm thinking about taking it up again," he said, shoving pipe and tobacco back in the desk drawer. He and his daughter shared a quiet moment. Danny didn't intervene. It took Barbara and her father a lot of years to learn to love one another again since her mother's death – a death she blamed her father for just as much as she blamed Bobby "Two Tone" Boyce.

"Do you want me to go?" Danny asked.

"And leave me alone here with him?" Barbara said with a smile in her eyes.

When the phone on the corner of the desk rang, Hartwell hesitated from picking it up, not seeming to want to ruin the moment he and his daughter shared. After four or five rings he snatched it up in his fist and said, "Hartwell here." He listened to the voice on the other end drawing his eyes up to Danny. He passed the receiver over, and said, "It's for you."

Danny took the receiver in his hand, shared a look with Barbara and her father before placing the phone to his ear and saying, "This is Brocko."

"It's me," Rosie DuBois said in a tight tone. "Can you meet me?"

Danny turned his back to Hartwell and Barbara before replying in a low tone, "Do you think that's wise?"

"I think Bobby is getting wise to my late nights with the girls," Rosie replied. "He's been in a state ever since his ledger was stollen. He's tightening security everywhere. Sooner or later, he's going to put a tail on me, if he hasn't already."

"Maybe it's best if we lay low for a while," Danny said.

Rosie was quiet on the other end, causing Danny to ask, "Are you still there?"

"I'm here," Rosie said in an annoyed tone. "I'm out on a limb. Sometimes the only way off it is to go forward. Are you going to meet me or not?"

Danny looked at his Timex, and said, "Alright, the usual place?"

Rosie let out a relieved sigh, and replied, "The usual place."

When Danny hung up the phone, Hartwell asked, "What was that all about?"

Danny collected his thoughts. Hartwell was his boss, but he worked for a higher purpose. Sometimes it was better if he didn't let Hartwell know everything. "I'm not sure," he finally said. "It might be something, it might be nothing."

"Who was that on the phone," Hartwell asked in a forceful tone.

"One of my contacts," was all Danny was willing to say as he broke eye contact with Hartwell, finding a pensive stare from Barbara.

Crossing the room, Danny stopped at the office door and said while picking up his hat from the table, "I'll let you know if I find anything out." He didn't give Hartwell time to say anything else as he pushed himself through the door and brazened up the corridor.

PART III

"You're late," the Purple Mystique said when Danny entered the Fleet Street warehouse, Mystique's base of operations.

"It couldn't be helped. I've had a busy twenty-four hours."

"It appears that way," Mystique said dismissively as she tinkered with her neutralizer weapon. "Any word on the street?"

"Nothing that you don't already know," Danny said.

"Then you haven't heard?" Mystique said clipping in the final part to upgrade her weapon.

Danny's eyes thinned, "Heard what?"

"Brother DaVivian is on the run," Mystique said sliding her gun into the folds of her coat.

"DaVivian is Two Tone's money launderer," Danny said.

"He's terrified what will happen to him if the ledger falls into the hands of the wrong people. I've been studying the book, and it seems DaVivian has his hands in thousands of dollars. Some of it counterfeit."

"If that's true, then Two Tone could flood the local economy with enough bogus notes to send the city... hell the whole country into a recession."

"Not what is needed after a worldwide depression," Mystique added. "We have to find him before Boyce. Two Tone won't want the man who knows about his finances being captured by the police."

"You think Boyce will have DaVivian killed?"

"Most probably," Mystique replied. "With the Ledger out of his control there's a good possibility Bobby Boyce will tie up any loose ends by silencing anyone who could rat on him. With DaVivian on the run, he knows it's only a matter of time before I or the police or Bobby "Two Tone" gets him. And it won't be long before others reported in that ledger get the same idea."

"Shouldn't we just turn over the ledger and let the authorities handle it?" Danny asked, but by the tone of his voice he already knew the answer.

"And have it tied up in red tape for years to come?" Mystique asked. "No. We deal with this our way. I'm willing to turn DaVivian over to the police when we find him, but the ledger stays with us. I'll hunt down everyone listed with in it and burn Boyce's empire down from the inside."

Danny squared himself on Mystique and asked, "You sure you know what you're doing?"

THE PURPLE MYSTIQUE

Mystique's eyes flashed red hot, and she said, "Was I wrong bringing you in on this with me, Danny?"

Before Danny could answer, Mystique stepped over his response, saying, "Because if I was, you need to tell me now."

"Are you saying you don't trust me?" Danny asked.

"I trusted you enough to share this with you," Mystique said.

"And I've kept your secret, and I always will until our job is finished."

Mystique drew a breath to say something, but now it was Danny's turn to step over her words, by saying, "But you have to promise me, you will finish this. That you're not playing games with Boyce. He's a smart man. Eventually he will figure out who the Purple Mystique is, and when he does, he'll burn *you* down."

"I became the Purple Mystique to see Boyce brought to justice," Mystique said. "The law is too slow in its due process. They have to be spoon fed the information, and then, then they will act more swiftly."

Danny reached out and took Mystique by the shoulders and squared her on him, and said, "Promise me... you have to promise me you have an end game to all this."

Mystique's face lightened and she said, "The ledger is the beginning of the end. We will use it to systematically unravel Boyce's operations. And that begins tonight, when we find Brother DaVivian."

Danny released his grip on her and stepped back. "Do you know where to start looking?" he asked.

"DaVivian covets prostitutes," Mystique said. "He's been known to find sanctuary in their bosom. His favorite is Madame Colette. If anything, she will know where to find him."

Danny eyed the purple Bentley, and then regarded Mystique.

"Are you driving for me tonight?" Mystique asked.

Danny crossed to the other side of the car and opened the driver side door. "Get in," he said. "We have a money launderer to hunt down."

There was a thunderstorm on the horizon, and a cool spring breeze blew chilly air off the lake. The zephyr ruffled the curtains in the suite apartment of Lady Colette. It was nearing eleven o'clock when the madame entered her apartment, her safe haven. She was the last of a dying breed. Her den of iniquity was founded during the conception of Chicago in the mid 1830s, and while there had been many others in the city, the original was still in operation. Though it had changed many locations over the decades, the Cascade Tower would be its last. Pressure from the city would spell the end to its one hundred plus years of operation, and soon it would fade into the annals of the city's vast history, though Colette understood many would see her whore house as a black stain on the Windy City.

She was a magnificent woman in her mid-sixties, with salt and pepper hair that was built into a tower atop her head. She wore heavy makeup in a vain attempt to hide the age lines splintering her features. Her dress was tight, and pushed her oversized breasts up firmly in hopes she would still be noticed over the young and virile women on her staff.

Pouring herself a glass of wine, she slipped out of her stilettos giving a relaxing groan as her bare feet sunk into the carpet underfoot. "I know you're here," she said when she took a drink from her glass. She turned as the Purple Mystique stepped out of the shadows. "I don't know where he is," Colette said. "Bobby Boyce inquired a few hours ago."

The Purple Mystique stepped further into the apartment and noticed the swelling on the left side of Colette's face. "Did he do that?" she asked nodding her head in indication of the welp.

Colette chuckled and said, "One of his oversized brutes. Bobby doesn't like getting his hands dirty."

"You're lucky he didn't do worse," Mystique said.

"And lose the chance of getting his rocks off any time he wishes?" Colette asked with a shake of her head. "Bobby Boyce knows not to muddy the waters he plays in."

"And what about Brother DaVivian?"

"I told you. I don't know where he is."

"Then you better give me some guesses, otherwise I'll do a hell of a lot worse than leave a welt on your face."

"And spoil your reputation as a champion for the citizens of Chicago. That's not your style at all," Colette said. "Look. If I knew where DaVivian was I'd tell you. Hell, I would have told Two Tone, but I simply don't know."

The Purple Mystique studied Colette for a fleeting second. The idea that she could have taken a hit to the face to throw her off DaVivian's scent was a possibility and when the door to the apartment exploded inward, that possibility became even more probable.

The room quickly filled with suit wearing thugs of Bobby "Two Tone" Boyce. They encircled the Purple Mystique, her only escape route was the window in which she entered, and luckily that was at her back, but she didn't make a break for it. Not yet. She came for answers, and she'd be damned if she left without them.

"I'm sorry my dear," Colette said. "But they had a suspicion you'd make an appearance."

Angelo "Sweet Face" Carmine came into the room a second later, a pistol in his hand and a smirk on his lips. "We meet again, Purple Mystique. Only this time I have the upper hand."

"Do you?" Mystique asked. "Nothing is always as it appears."

"The ledger, where is it?" Sweet face snapped.

Mystique's wide brim fedora masked most of her features, but only her purple stained lips were seen curving up into a smile. "It's someplace safe, out of your reach, and that's where it will remain."

Enraged, Sweet Face stormed forward, his gun out in front of him. "I could kill you now."

"You could," Mystique said. "But you can't risk the ledger falling into the hands of the police if I die, now, can you?"

"You're damned arrogant," Sweet Face snarled.

"And you're damned stupid if you think I came into this room unprepared," Mystique said as she clutched two round bobbles in her right hand. Throwing strength into her arm, she raised the rubbery devices into the air and smashed them against the floor expelling her amethyst gas into the room. The mist enveloped the armed thugs sending them into a coughing frenzy – temporarily blinding them. The Purple Mystique dashed across the room toward Madame Colette who had gone to her knees choking on the vapor.

Mystique forced the madame back to her feet and pushed her against the wall away from the toxic ether. Taking Colette's head into her hands, she squared the woman's eyes on her and said, "You know where Brother DaVivian is, don't you?"

Under the influence of the gas, Colette nodded, and said, "He's no longer in the city. He's on a ship in the lake, two miles out. The *Horafax*. It's preparing to make sail at daybreak."

"And does Two Tone know?" Mystique asked.

"I told him an hour ago. I had no other choice," Colette said. "He threatened to hurt my girls if I didn't tell him."

"Listen to me," Mystique said. "You will remember nothing of my presence here, nor of Sweet Face and his men. Do you understand me?"

Colette nodded signifying her understanding.

The Purple Mystique turned toward Sweet Face. The scarred-face man succumbed to the amethyst gas, but he remained on his feet, mesmerized – the irises of his eyes were enlarged and susceptible. Under the control of the toxic mist Mystique could command anyone weak-minded enough to adhere to her commands. For a fleeting second, she considered ordering Sweet Face and his men to turn themselves into the police. But once out of the gas' control he might circumvent any orders given him. She would have to bury an order deep in his subconscious, one that would remain and fester until triggered.

With a wave of her hand, Mystique drew Sweet Face to her, and she allowed their eyes to meet. In a spellbinding tone she kept her voice level and controlling. "You will forget I was here, you forget what I look like, and you will forget you were even here. When asked, you will become belligerent and uncontrollable, rage will take control, and you will have no idea why you are acting in such a state. Do you understand?"

Sweet Face nodded his understanding, and Mystique said, "Now go, go and don't look back."

It was a gamble. Most people under hypnosis were less likely to go against their nature when an idea was planted within their mind, but the amethyst gas was much more powerful than any power a carnival hypnotist might have.

Glancing back at Colette who remained in her hypnotic state, an idea crossed the Purple Mystique's mind, but she refrained from acting. Any suggestion she might give the Madame, would go against her own moral code, the code she imposed on herself when she began her battle against Bobby Boyce. Colette was not an evil person, she did what was right by her and Mystique couldn't hold that against her. As she slipped out the window, Mystique said, "Sleep, Lady Colette. Sleep and awake refreshed."

Danny Brocko piloted a boat over the turbulent waters of Lake Michigan well after midnight. He switched off the small motor at the back of the boat as they neared the merchant vessel *Horafax*, masking their arrival. An anchor chain stretched out from the ship disappearing into the murky lake water as the Purple Mystique reached out for it and hoisted herself up.

"You sure you don't want me to come?" Danny asked as he clutched the anchor chain and steadied the small craft.

Mystique looked back toward her friend and said, "I'll move stealthier alone, but if I'm not back in a half hour..."

"I'll come get you," Danny insisted.

"No," Mystique snapped. "You'll call the Coast Guard..."

"And tell them what?"

"I don't know," Mystique said as she continued her climb. "Make something up but do whatever you can to prevent this ship from getting away."

Danny said something else, but Mystique couldn't hear him as she concentrated and moved up. Stopping less than a minute later, she peered over the railing investigating the deck. She saw no one and pulled herself up – keeping low as she moved into the dark. There were little pinpoints of light dotting the surface as she took quiet steps.

If Brother DaVivian was on the ship, he was most likely below deck, and that's where she needed to go. When she heard approaching footsteps, she drew herself back into an alcove watching and waiting as two men came into view. They stopped inches from her hiding place, peering out into the black waters. *Danny,* she thought. Had the crew seen them approach? She quickly dismissed that idea, for if they had been seen, there would be more than two unarmed men staring out at the lake.

"Are you sure you heard the transmission, right?" the taller of the two men asked.

"I can only tell you what I heard," the shorter stout man said. "Said Bobby Boyce was onboard and heading this way."

In the distance the lights of an approaching boat grew brighter as the craft came closer.

"What should we do?"

"Do? We do nothing, that's what we do," the taller man said. "This ship belongs to Bobby Boyce, I fancy myself staying alive, and by doing so, I don't piss off the man who can send me to the bottom of the lake with cement loafers."

Suddenly a thick fog rolled off Lake Michigan shrouding Boyce's boat – as if heralding his arrival. The *Horafax* swayed gently at anchor, but the air was going steadily colder. Even shrouded in her long flowing trench coat, Mystique felt the air's brisk sting. It was the perfect setting for a murder and its victim, Brother DaVivian was waiting his fate somewhere down below.

"Let's go meet him," the taller man said. "But keep your trap shut. Boyce likes to only hear yes, Sir when he talks. So, let me do the replying."

"I understand, Skipper."

Mystique came out of her hiding place and leaned against the cold steel of the ship's railing, her eyes scanning the foggy horizon for the arrival of the other vessel. She adjusted her fedora, pulling the brim low over her eyes.

A low rumble in the distance caught her attention. The fog parted slightly, revealing the silhouette of another ship, creeping silently toward the *Horafax*. No doubt filled with

Boyce's goons, ready to claim DaVivian for themselves. Time was running out.

When another crewman came out of nowhere, Mystique acted quickly, pouncing on the man with a swift fluid motion as if she had been practicing for the encounter. Producing a knife from the folds of her coat, she placed it to the man's throat and warned, "If you want to live through this night, you'll tell me what I need to know."

The crewman nodded nervously, and Mystique said, "Where is Brother DaVivian?"

Mystique moved quickly, her heels clicking softly on the deck as she made her way toward the lower levels of the ship. DaVivian was hidden away in a storage compartment below deck, and Mystique wasted no time. Boyce and his men were onboard, and it was only a matter of time, and they would be wolfs on her heels.

She reached the door to the compartment and paused, listening. Satisfied no one was inside with DaVivian, she turned the latch and entered the quarters.

DaVivian lay on a shoddy looking cot, fully dressed in a crisp gray suit, right down to his finely polished black shoes. He looked up as Mystique entered, his eyes filled with a mixture of anger and fear, he swung his legs over the side of the cot and sat up, only to be kicked back when Mystique shoved her high heels into his chest.

"It's true what they say about you. You have a flair for the dramatic," DaVivian sneered, his voice surprisingly jovial.

Mystique ignored him. "You know why I'm here," she said. "You're in deep with Boyce."

"That's why I'm on this ship," DaVivian said. "Getting out of town seemed the smart thing to do."

"Your plan would have worked too, if Lady Colette didn't give you up," Mystique said.

DaVivian tried to sit up, but Mystique's foot didn't waver. "Now see here," he said. His seraph eyes and angelic features did not waver, and it was the first time Mystique really took a good look at him. He was handsome, almost too handsome to the point he looked fake, as if he worked hard to make himself look other worldly. "I work for Bobby Boyce, he wouldn't kill me."

"What if we just wait here and see what he does when he comes through that door," Mystique said. "I'm giving you a chance to survive this, DaVivian. But you need to trust me."

He eyed Mystique warily, as if he was trying to decide if what she told him was the truth. With suspicion in his eyes, he asked, "Why should I trust you?"

"Because right now I'm all you have," she said firmly. "And I'm the only one who can get you out of this alive."

For a moment, he said nothing, the tension between them thick as the fog outside. Then, with a resigned sigh, DaVivian nodded, and Mystique removed her foot from his chest.

DaVivian rubbed his chest, wincing. He stood, but before he could say anything more, the sound of boots clattering on the deck above made them both freeze. Boyce's men had arrived.

THE PURPLE MYSTIQUE

"We need to move," Mystique whispered, grabbing DaVivian's arm and pulling him toward the door. But before they could reach it, the door burst open, and two of Boyce's goons stepped inside, guns drawn.

"Well, well, what do we have here?" one of them sneered, his eyes darting between Mystique and DaVivian. "The Purple Mystique and the traitor himself. Boss is going to be real happy when we bring you two in."

Mystique's heart pounded in her chest, but she didn't show it. Instead, she smiled coldly. "I wouldn't count on it." In a flash, she spiraled a roundhouse kick, her foot striking the nearest goon's wrist, forcing him to drop his gun. Before he could react, she grabbed the weapon and aimed it at the other goon, firing a single shot it struck him in the leg crippling him. The goon let out a painful yelp and crumpled to the floor.

The first goon, now disarmed, lunged at her, but Mystique was faster. She sidestepped his attack and brought the butt of the gun down on the back of his head, knocking him out cold.

"Let's go," she hissed, pulling DaVivian out of the compartment and back into the corridor. "They surely heard that shot."

The ship was a maze of narrow passageways and steep staircases, and Mystique used her instincts well. She led DaVivian through the winding corridors, always keeping one step ahead of the approaching footsteps behind them. They reached the deck just as more of Boyce's men appeared, but Mystique had a plan.

She dragged DaVivian to the edge of the ship near the anchor, where the small motorboat was masked in the darkened fog. The inky water looked like a silk curtain flowing with a mind of its own. "Dan, you there?" Mystique inquired.

"You better hope so," Danny shot back. "You're about to be overrun by a group of hoods."

Mystique turned to see a mass of bodies flowing in her direction. She grabbed DaVivian by the scruff of the neck and said, "Climb down and get in the boat."

"Boat, what boat?" DaVivian asked, "There's nothing there."

"It's there," Mystique assured him as she pulled her amethyst gun from inside her jacket.

DaVivian looked over the railing again but shook his head in refusal. "You're a crazy dame," he said.

"Danny, time to go fishing," Mystique said shoving DaVivian over the edge; he let out a horrified scream as he tumbled to the waves below. "Did you get him?" she asked.

"Talk about the big one that almost got away," Danny shouted, and added, "I got'em!"

Before Mystique could throw her leg over the railing, two large arms wrapped around her in a boa constrictor squeeze. She dropped her gas gun as she reached behind her, grabbing at anything she could. With only seconds before she was pounced upon by a horde of goons, Mystique acted fast. Using all the strength she had available, she turned her body just enough to shove her thumb into her attacker's right eye. She dug it in deep, and her gloved hand became saturated with warm liquid.

THE PURPLE MYSTIQUE

The man screamed and he released her, as Mystique dropped to her feet. She knelt scooping up her amethyst gun and shoving it back in her coat, as she leapt over the side of the railing, dropping, dropping, dropping until she hit the icy waters of the Michigan.

Seconds later Danny's hand grabbed her, and he hoisted her into the boat. Hacking the murky water from her lungs, she said, "Get us out of here...!" as gun fire came from above.

The motor roared to life, and the boat shot away from the *Horafax*, disappearing into the fog. "Keep down," Mystique insisted as she pulled DaVivian out of harm's way. Bullets whizzed past them, but the cover of the mist was on their side and masked their escape.

As the sound of gunfire faded behind them, DaVivian slumped back in the boat, breathing heavily. "What now?" he asked, his voice laced with exhaustion.

Mystique didn't answer immediately. She kept her eyes on the horizon, with Danny steering the boat toward the distant lights of Chicago.

"Now," she finally said, "We get you somewhere safe. And then, you're going to tell the police everything you know about Boyce."

DaVivian nodded, too tired to argue. "And what about you?"

A small smile tugged at the corner of her lips. "I'll be fine. The Purple Mystique always lands on her feet."

As the lights of Chicago drew nearer, the fog lifted, unveiling the city skyline. The Purple Mystique understood the road ahead would be challenging, but she was confident in her decision. She could have exploited DaVivian for her own vendetta against Bobby Boyce, but she chose to prioritize the greater good over her own ambitions. Revenge would come, but it would take time. Danny's words echoed in her mind—Boyce was sharp and would eventually uncover her true identity. She needed to be prepared, knowing that the revelation of the Purple Mystique's alter ego would ultimately shock everyone.

Who is the *Purple Mystique*?
Is it Lena "Velvet" Thompson
the singer at the Silver Key?

Or is it Bobby "Two Tone" Boyce's squeeze
Rosie DuBois?

Maybe it's district attorney
William Hartwell's daughter, Barbara.

All three have a vendetta towards Bobby Boyce, but only one of them can be...
The *Purple Mystique*...
Who do you think it is?
More Purple Mystique adventures coming soon.

ABOUT THE AUTHOR

Charles F. Millhouse is an Award-Winning Author and Publisher. He published his first book in 1999 and he hasn't looked back. Having written over thirty books in the Pulp/Science Fiction genres. His imagination is boundless. From the 1930's adventures of Captain Hawklin – through the gritty paranormal old west town of New Kingdom – to the far-off future in the Origin Trilogy, Charles breathes life into his characters, brings worlds alive and sends his readers on journeys they won't soon forget.

Charles lives in Southeastern, Ohio with his wife and two sons.

Visit stormgatepress.com for more details.

Printed in Great Britain
by Amazon